EXTRA!
EXTRA!
Fairy-Tale News
from Hidden Forest

UNITED STATES
MÉXICO
Pacific Ocean
ITALY
EDITORIAL
El Mundo
MAPS
Herbs
Zucchini
CORN
Peppers
Lettuce

EXTRA! EXTRA!

Fairy-Tale News from Hidden Forest

by Alma Flor Ada
illustrated by Leslie Tryon

ATHENEUM BOOKS FOR YOUNG READERS New York • London • Toronto • Sydney

To my daughter-in-law, Denise Zubizarreta, and
my grandchildren, Timothy Paul, Samantha Rose, and Victoria.
It was fun brainstorming this book with you!
And to little Nicholas, for the joy he brings us all.
—A. F. A.

For two extra, extra special boys, Alexandros and Liam.
—L. T.

· ACKNOWLEDGMENTS ·

Thanks to Alison Velea for her insightful comments,
and to Kristy Raffensberger, a true fairy-tale editor!

Atheneum Books for Young Readers
An imprint of Simon & Schuster Children's Publishing Division
1230 Avenue of the Americas, New York, New York 10020

Book design by Debra Sfetsios and Krista Vossen
The text for this book is set in Letterpress Text.
The illustrations for this book are rendered in pen and ink, watercolor, and Prismacolor pencil.
Manufactured in China
First Edition
2 4 6 8 10 9 7 5 3 1
CIP data for this book is available from the Library of Congress.
ISBN-13: 978-0-689-82582-8
ISBN-10: 0-689-82582-X

NEWS
Causes
HIDDEN MEADOW
HIDDEN

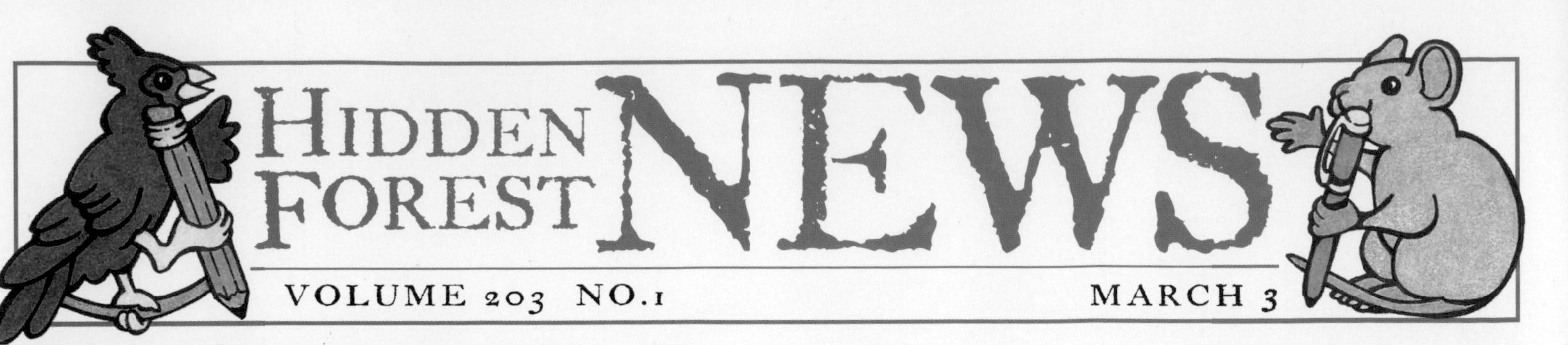

HIDDEN FOREST NEWS
VOLUME 203 NO.1
MARCH 3

Mysterious Plant Causes Alarm

HIDDEN MEADOW—A huge vine, resembling an oversized beanstalk that reaches the clouds, seems to have grown overnight and is alarming residents in this quiet area of Hidden Forest.

"No such thing should be allowed to grow," expressed Mr. McGregor, the longtime owner of McGregor's Farm. "Nothing good can come of this. Beans are not supposed to grow this tall."

No one knows what caused the plant to appear or to grow to its present size. "It's a danger to us all," said Mrs. Bear, whose residence is close to the place where the plant suddenly sprouted. "I have spent all day watching over Baby Bear, who is determined to climb up that plant. Have you noticed that it grows as if it were a stairway? Heaven only knows where it goes! A person could get killed falling off it!"

"Nothing good can come of this. Beans are not supposed to grow this tall."

The closest neighbors to the giant beanstalk, Mrs. Blake and her son, Jack, were not at home and could not be questioned about this unusual plant.

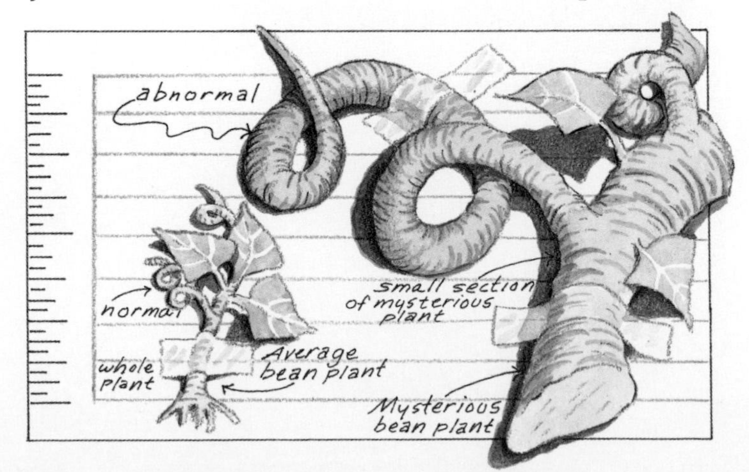

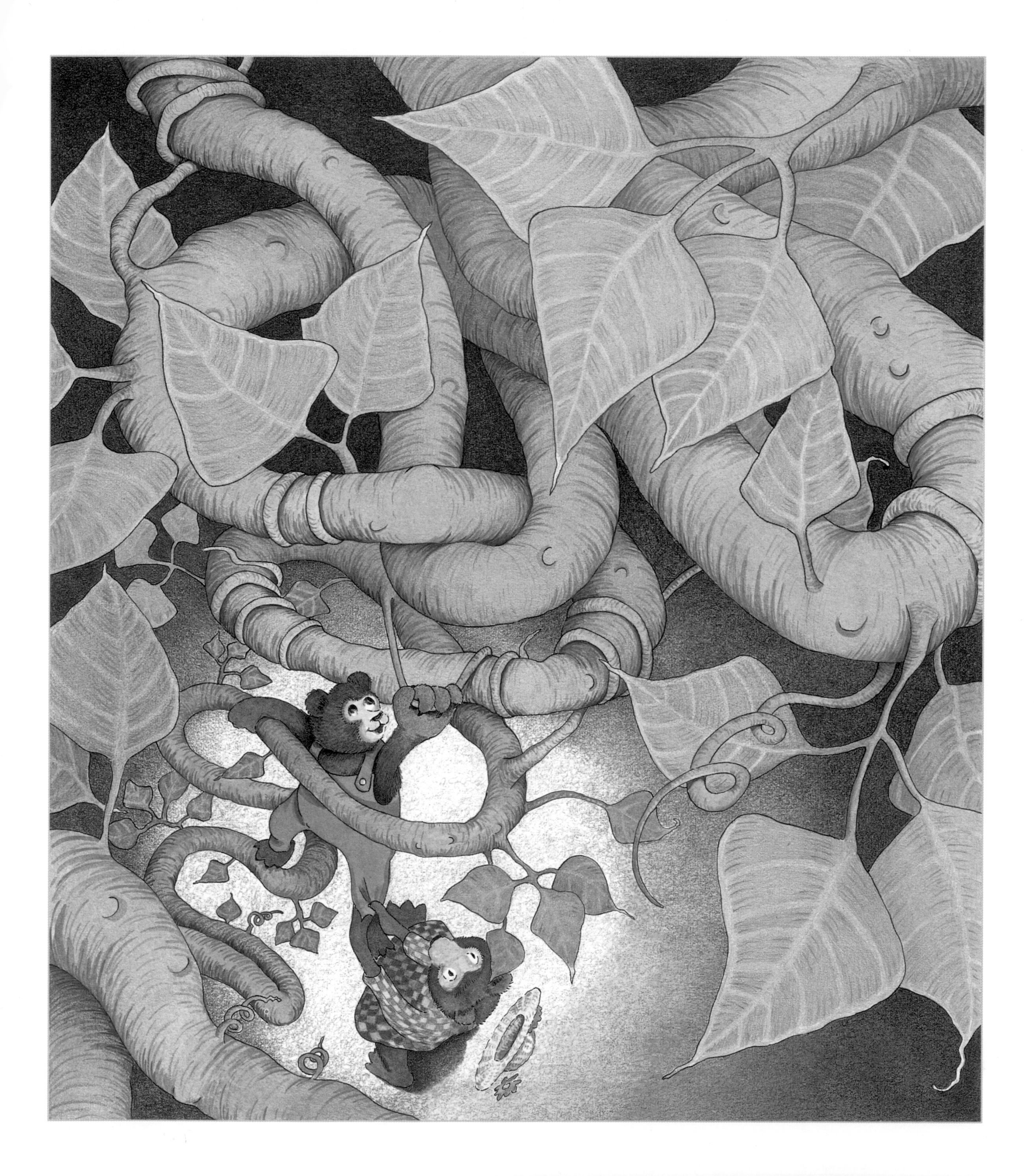

A GROWING MENACE!

by L. Feline, aka Mr. Cat

Many Hidden Forest neighbors have expressed their desire to get rid of the strange plant that has mysteriously appeared in Hidden Meadow.

"Anything we don't understand is dangerous." This was the opinion of Mr. Wolfy Lupus, seconded by his cousin, Mr. Fer O'Cious, who proposed that the plant be chopped down immediately.

Others fear that a crop from such giant beanstalks could be detrimental to the agricultural business of the area. Mr. McGregor summed up the issue: "This plant is unfair competition. It could produce more beans than my whole field."

We support the idea of eliminating the threat. Let's continue our lives as we always have. Let's get rid of the menace!

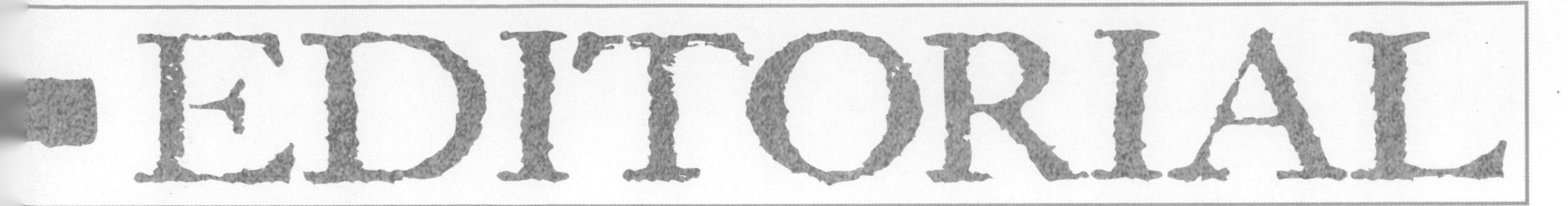

THERE'S RICHNESS IN DIVERSITY

by Hetty Henny

Being new and different doesn't necessarily mean that something is bad. The world is full of wonders waiting to be discovered.

At the present moment Hidden Forest has the opportunity to explore a new species. We know that many new medicines can be extracted from plants. What if this surprising plant has the power to cure an illness? Could it, with its potentially large crop, be an answer to hunger and famine in the world?

Our planet is rich in its diversity. There is not just one flower, but many of them: roses, violets, carnations, lilies. There is not just one fish, but many of them, from sharks to goldfish. Why shouldn't there be all kinds of beans?

We should wait and learn more about this plant before making a final decision.

INTERNATIONAL

Italian Village Concerned About Fate of Beloved Toy Maker

ITALY—The toy shop of Mr. Geppetto has given joy to generations of children. An artist of great talent and craftsmanship, Mr. Geppetto is renowned for his wooden puppets, carved so realistically that they seem to be alive.

The closing of his toy shop has brought about much concern. No one has heard from Mr. Geppetto since last Tuesday. Neighbors suggest that the toy maker may have gone in search of Pinocchio, a puppet he carved and looked after as if it were his own son. Pinocchio left for school on Monday morning and never returned home. The children of the town have taken up a collection to offer as a reward for anyone who can provide news of their beloved toy maker and his puppet.

Amazing Chick Sets Out to Visit Capital

MÉXICO—The unique Half-Chicken, born on a farm on the outskirts of Guadalajara with just one leg, one wing, and one eye, has set out to visit the capital city of México.

When asked by our reporter why he wanted to undertake such a long trip, he answered, "I have been told I'm unique. Everyone says the capital city is unique. I want to see what makes us alike."

UNUSUAL RACE

A surprising race between the Hare and the Tortoise has been announced for tomorrow. Most bystanders interviewed by our reporter believe the Tortoise has no possibility at all of winning this uneven race. But there are some among the crowd who have expressed their support for the Tortoise as a very resilient and resourceful individual.

Poll %	TORTOISE		HARE	
100 / 50 / 0	will win	won't win	will win	won't win

Discover the hidden poet in *you*! Send us four lines that give us your opinion of our newspaper. The winning entry will be published in an upcoming issue.

FIRST PRIZE:

a delicious carrot cake

donated by
Mrs. Josephine Rabbit

BACK PAGE

FUR

Enjoy the luxury of
a furry look—instantly!
Patches Ears Tails
Faux furs custom made
to your needs.
Speedy Raccoon, Faux Furrier
Forest Drive, Hidden Forest

TAG SALE

Large assortment of binoculars,
eyeglasses, and telescopes

Mr. Fer O'Cious
Majestic Tower,
Hidden Lane
Wooden Heights

BRICKLAYING • MASONRY LANDSCAPING

Enrich your life with a stone fireplace.
Beautify your home.

- Outdoor Ovens
- Brick Paths

Careful, detailed
construction

Pig Three, Mason
Brick House, Woodsy Woods

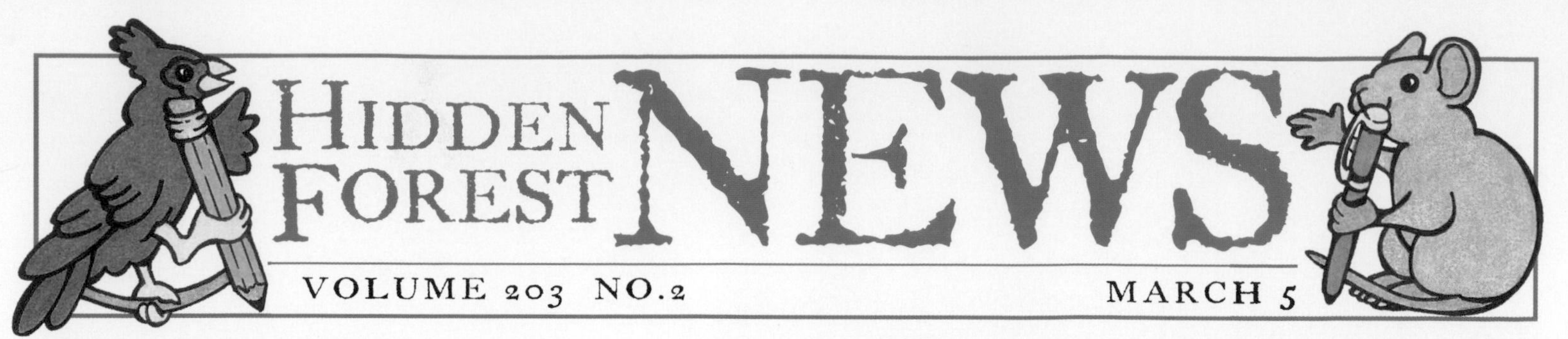
HIDDEN FOREST NEWS
VOLUME 203 NO.2 MARCH 5

Disappearance of Boy Linked to Mystery Plant

Jack, shown above, with family cow.

HIDDEN MEADOW—Jack, the only son of Mrs. Blake, was last seen standing under the giant beanstalk that grew across the road from the Blake home. His disappearance seems to be connected with the huge plant, which has alarmed many residents of Hidden Forest.

"Jack has always been a good boy," said Mrs. Blake. "Although last Sunday he made me very upset when he traded our only cow for a bunch of beans, he always tries to do the right thing. I don't want to believe he has climbed up that plant, but he has never been gone this long before. Since he didn't come home last night I haven't been able to stop worrying."

While the neighbors demand that the plant be chopped down, Mrs. Blake insists it should stay. "I won't let anybody take this plant down," she said. "If Jack is up there, he'll need this plant to come back home."

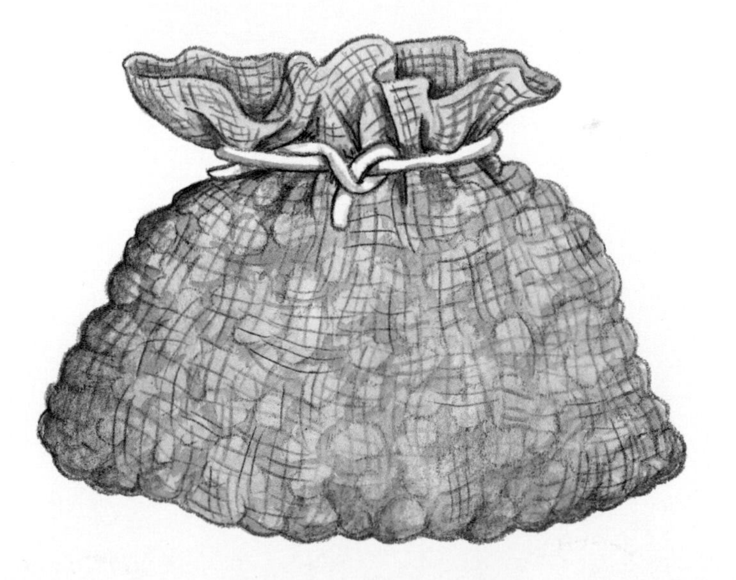
Beans traded for cow.

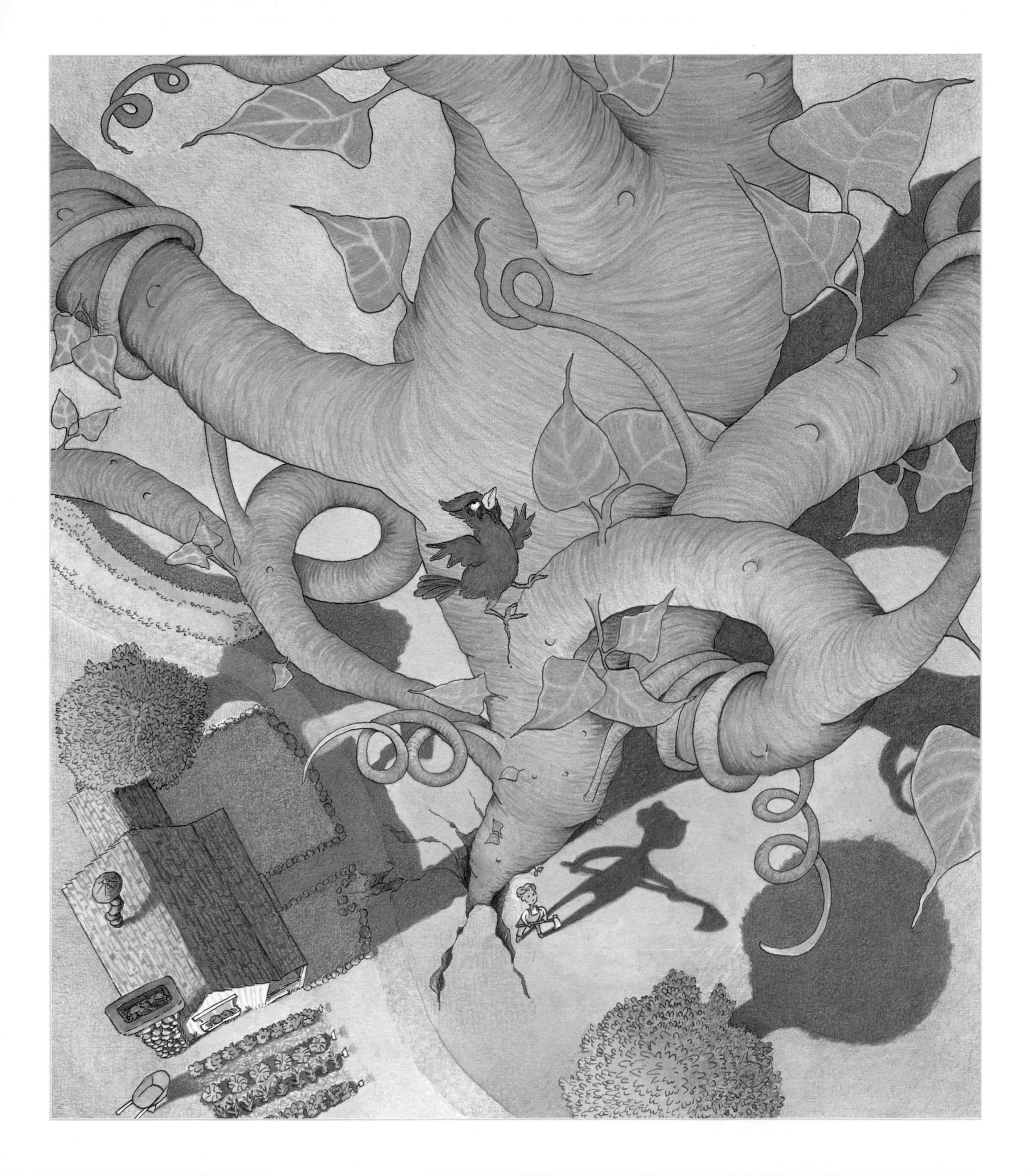

GET RID OF THE THREATENING PLANT!

by L. Feline, aka Mr. Cat

The Hidden Forest neighbors who have proposed to chop down the unsightly plant that has invaded our community are convinced that they are right in calling it a threat. The disappearance of young Jack Blake is proof of the danger of the giant beanstalk.

"What would happen to our community," demanded Mr. Fer O'Cious, "if all young delicious morsels climb up that godforsaken vine? What will be left for respectable citizens like me to pursue?"

Good question. It may not be long before ambitious citizens like Mr. Fer O'Cious and Mr. Wolfy Lupus take it upon themselves to bring down the encroaching plant. How many more youngsters need to disappear before we recognize the danger? Let's get rid of the menace now!

IT'S A FOOLISH DEBATE—WE MUST WAIT

by Hetty Henny

The large beanstalk is a magnificent sight to see. It is a reminder that giants live on our planet, sometimes in distant places like the towering redwoods and the majestic sequoias. Instead of being threatened by their size, we should stand in admiration of them. After all, we too seem giant to other living things. But we must all live in harmony.

There is also another reason for not cutting down the beanstalk: A mother awaits the return of her son. He disappeared a few days ago and she believes that he climbed the plant. How could we destroy his only means of coming home? We do not want to break up this happy family!

There is talk of a search party planning to scale the stalk. It would be a dangerous mission, but Jack Blake must be found.

Where is Geppetto?

Return of the Puppet Pinocchio Clouded by Geppetto's Absence

ITALY—The puppet Pinocchio, who was missing for some time, returned yesterday to an empty home. A note left by Mr. Geppetto indicated that the toy maker was planning to make a raft and sail in search of his beloved son.

Our correspondent approached Pinocchio as he stood watching the ocean from a high cliff. "Poor Father, I will find him," were his only words.

The uncertain fate of Mr. Geppetto has brought concern to many children, who are keeping lighted candles in their windows as a message of hope.

Half-Chicken Stops Along the Way to Show His Kindness

MÉXICO—The reporter covering Half-Chicken's trip to the capital city of México reports that Half-Chicken is not only a unique-looking creature, but also a kind one. Although he is very intent on completing his trip and won't stop for sightseeing or recreation, he has made several stops along his way to come to the aid of Wind, Fire, and Water. They will surely not forget him.

SPORTS

Surprising Results of Yesterday's Race

To the shock of most of the observers of yesterday's race, it was not the favorite, Hare, who won the bet, but the resilient and resourceful Tortoise!

NOTICE

• Important Meeting •

Let's gather together to discuss
the giant beanstalk's future.
We should come to a decision
as a community.
All opinions are welcome.

Meet at Community Hall
March 10, 7:00 p.m.

Cooperative Farming

Join us in establishing a Farming Co-op and a Farmers' Market. Working together, we will achieve greater results.

· POTLUCK ·

Next Thursday at 6:00 p.m.
at Ms. Red Hen's house
Avenue of the Elms, Happy Valley
Child care with entertainment provided
courtesy of Goldilocks and
Little Red Riding Hood

BACK PAGE

Cooking Lessons

Finger-licking recipes

• • •

SPECIALIZING IN CHICKEN

All classes with a banquet!
We provide the instructions.
You provide the ingredients.

Wolfy Lupus
Wolf Lane, Oakshire

Papa Bear's
BIRDHOUSES
All Handmade
SPECIAL OFFER
One bag
of birdseed
FREE*
*with the purchase of a birdhouse

WE TREAT ALL YOUR AILMENTS

Experienced an unfortunate accident?
Snared in your own traps?

We'll take care of you.

Turkey Lurkey, MD
Resident Physician
Ailments Road, Hidden Forest

EXTRA

EXTRA

EXTRA

EXTRA

HIDDEN FOREST NEWS INTERNATIONAL

Toy Maker Geppetto
His Son Pinocchio
nited in the
ils of a Whale

them to a neighboring village
assistance. He reports that fathe
son were delighted
to be alive and made
mention of finding
each other in the
entrails of a huge
whale. This amazing
story could not be confirmed by our
reporter because he arrived in the village
after Mr. Geppetto and Pinocchio had
started their journey home.

HIDDEN FOREST NEWS INTERNATIONAL # EXTRA

Toy Maker Geppetto and His Son Pinocchio Reunited in the Entrails of a Whale

ITALY—A surprised fisherman found the toy maker Mr. Geppetto, who had disappeared for many days, and his son, Pinocchio, lying exhausted on a shore next to the remains of a makeshift raft. The fisherman took them to a neighboring village for assistance. He reports that father and son were delighted to be alive and made mention of finding each other in the entrails of a huge whale. This amazing story could not be confirmed by our reporter because he arrived in the village after Mr. Geppetto and Pinocchio had already started their journey home.

Although stories of whales swallowing people surface occasionally, whales usually do not attack ships or human beings.

HALF-CHICKEN EXPERIENCING TERRIBLE ORDEAL

MÉXICO—The reporter who has been shadowing Half-Chicken since the beginning of his trip witnessed the unique chicken disappearing through the back door of the viceroy's palace. Through the kitchen window our reporter saw Half-Chicken in the hands of the vice-royal cook, who seemed determined to throw him in a pot of boiling water. The reporter tried to enter the viceroy's palace, but he was refused admittance by the vice-royal guards.

This would be a terrible ending for such a brave, kind chicken.

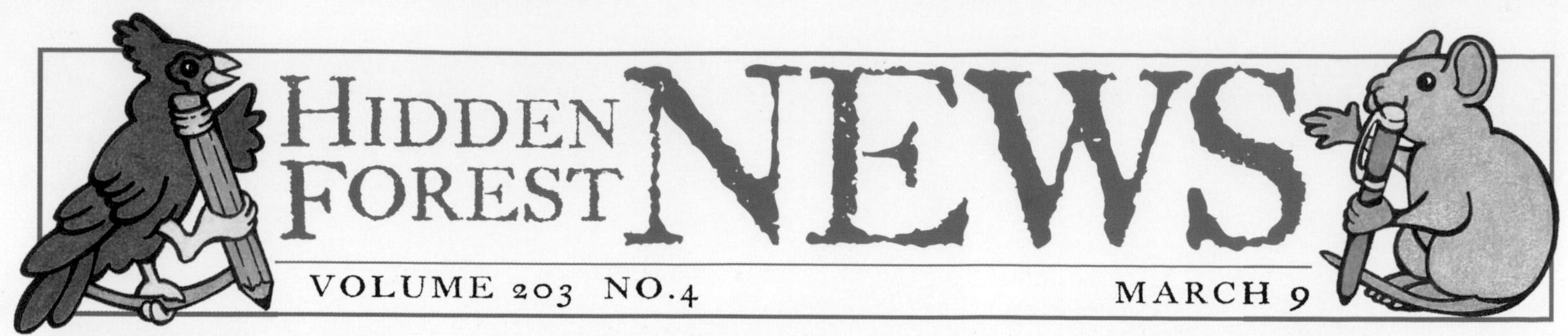

HIDDEN FOREST NEWS
VOLUME 203 NO.4
MARCH 9

END OF HIDDEN FOREST FEAR

Giant Returns to the Clouds

HIDDEN MEADOW—The plant that has brought so much distress to this community was finally removed, and the young boy who disappeared has been restored to his family today.

Eight days ago an enormous beanstalk sprouted here. No one seemed to know where it came from. Hidden Forest neighbors held different opinions about what should be done with the plant. But, in spite of the many individuals who wanted to chop it down, Mrs. Blake of Hidden Meadow prevailed in protecting the plant. She believed her son, Jack, had disappeared by climbing it, and she wanted him to have a way to return home.

After spending two days and two nights at the foot of the giant beanstalk, holding an ax to discourage anyone from chopping it down, Mrs. Blake received her reward: Her son, Jack, finally climbed down. He was very frightened and yelled to his mother that a giant was following him, so Mrs. Blake quickly cut down the beanstalk.

Mrs. Blake claims that she saw the head of the giant among the clouds and heard him shouting loudly. Because a major thunderstorm rolled in at that moment, some neighbors prefer to believe that all she saw and heard was thunder and lightning. We may never find out the entire truth about this mystery, but we join the residents of Hidden Forest in welcoming Jack home.

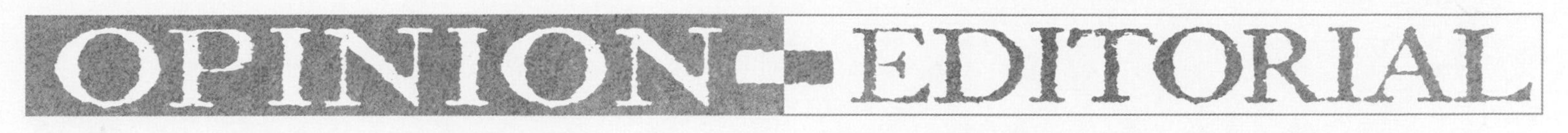

FINALLY RID OF THE MENACE!

by L. Feline, aka Mr. Cat

At last we are rid of the menace that has shattered the peace in Hidden Forest. The giant that Mrs. Blake heard shouting down among the clouds is final proof that the plant should never have been allowed to stand for even one day. Imagine what destruction could have ensued if that giant had climbed down and unleashed his power!

We must learn from this. I understand that some neighbors have collected beans from the dangerous beanstalk. I urge you not to plant them!

L. Feline, aka Mr. Cat

WE WAITED AND FOUND OUT

by Hetty Henny

Violence and destruction are not sensible ways to bring about solutions. An unjustified attack can cause much sorrow. Mrs. Blake taught us all a great lesson when she insisted on preserving the beanstalk. Should the plant have been cut down, as some ill-advised individuals proposed, her son, Jack, would have been lost forever.

Hetty Henny

Instead he is now happily reunited with his mother and has brought a valuable gift for the community.

It is a shame that the magnificent vine had to come down in the end because everyone was afraid of the giant. But since it was allowed to grow to full maturity, and its beans have been preserved, there are plans to initiate a crop that may provide ample food for needy creatures in the future.

INTERNATIONAL

First Weather Vane Atop Tower of Viceroy's Palace in Mexico City

MÉXICO—Kindness received its just reward. Half-Chicken, whose trip to the capital city of México has been followed by one of our reporters, was saved from a terrible end. When the vice-royal cook threw Half-Chicken into a pot of water on the fire, Water and Fire remembered the strange creature's kindness and came to his rescue. Water spilled on Fire, who immediately allowed itself to be extinguished. When the cook threw Half-Chicken, now useless to him, out of the window, Wind lifted him up to the top of the highest tower. From there the unique chicken will have the best view of the capital city and the company of his friend, Wind.

PINOCCHIO AND GEPPETTO RETURN HOME, GREETED WITH GREAT ENTHUSIASM

ITALY—The toy maker Mr. Geppetto has returned home a very happy man. He was accompanied by Pinocchio, a puppet he carved out of wood and kept as a son. Pinocchio seems to have undergone an extraordinary transformation: He is now a real boy of flesh and bone. Both father and son were too weary to make lengthy declarations after their ordeal.

"We are just happy to be home," said Mr. Geppetto.

"Our greatest joy is being together," added Pinocchio.

The children of the village are planning a major celebration in honor of Mr. Geppetto and Pinocchio.

JACK SPEAKS OUT

Exclusive Interview with Jack About His Beanstalk Adventure

by Bonnie Longears

Ms. Longears: Jack, you've had a harrowing ordeal. Would you please tell us about your adventure with the giant beanstalk? When was the first time you saw this plant?

Jack: The morning after I traded our cow for some magic beans.

Ms. Longears: You traded a cow for beans? How did that come about?

Jack: Our life has been difficult since my father died. A cow was all we had left, and we had no money for food. So my mother asked me to take the cow and sell it at the market.

Ms. Longears: And then what happened?

Jack: I met a most interesting old gentleman. He assured me that if I traded him the cow for some magic beans, I would make my fortune.

Ms. Longears: Your fortune? I see. So, what then?

Jack: My mother got upset with me and threw the magic beans out the window. One of them must have sprouted and grew into the giant beanstalk.

Ms. Longears: Did you ever make your fortune?

Jack: I had a difficult adventure. But I was able to bring back a goose that lays golden eggs. My mother and I have decided to donate the hen to the community. Hopefully it will lay enough eggs to build a community center.

Ms. Longears: That's a generous gesture, Jack. Everyone in Hidden Forest will be thankful. It must make you very happy.

Jack: I'm even happier thinking about the crops that may come out of the beans I just planted.

Ms. Longears: Thank you, Jack. Best wishes to you.

Jack: Good-bye, Ms. Longears. Best wishes to all *Hidden Forest News* readers.

...and grew into the GIANT beanstalk.
News

SUMMER CAMP FOR CHILDREN

Once-in-a-lifetime experiences!
Adventures never to be repeated!
Entrust your children to us—
they will never be the same!

Mr. Fer O'Cious and Mr. Wolfy Lupus,
Directors

Majestic Tower,
Hidden Lane Wooden Heights

BEAUTIFUL CLOTHES FOR CHILDREN

Comfortable • Durable • All-natural materials
Most colors available: blue, green, yellow, purple (No requests for red, please.)
Grandma Rose Redding, Cottage in the Woods, Hidden Forest

Vegetarian Meals

Delicacies from the Meadow

Wholesomely prepared by Mother Rabbit
Soups, Salads, Casseroles, Desserts

. . .

HOUSE SPECIALTIES:
Carrot Soup, Carrot Salad, Carrot Cake

Rhyming CONTEST

Thanks to all the readers who submitted entries.

HERE IS THE WINNING RHYME:

Hidden Forest News
We follow the news day and night
We tell you all, we tell it right.
We're the best, we find the clues
We're *Hidden Forest News*!

And remember, you do not need a contest to send your contributions to *Hidden Forest News*. This is your newspaper! Your words are always welcome!

Editor and Publisher: *Grandma Rose Redding*
International Writer: *Papa Bear*
Gardening Expert: *Mr. McGregor*
Typeset, Layout, and Classifieds: *Little Red Hen*
Photography: *Little Red Riding Hood*
Press Room: *Pig One and Pig Two*
Op-Ed Contributors: *L. Feline and Hetty Henny*
Press Room Assistant: *Baby Bear*
Distribution and Delivery: *Peter Rabbit*
Copy Runners: *Red Hen's chicks*

NEWS

ACK PAGE
NEWS
ACK PAGE

Inter
First W
toptower of
Palace In
MÉXICO—
... and
into